PRESENTED TO

_____

FROM

_____

A Story of
Easter
and All of Us

Roma Downey & Mark Burnett

Faith
Words

New York | Boston | Nashville

Copyright © 2014 by Lightworkers Media

All rights reserved. In accordance with the U.S. Copyright Act of 1976, the scanning,
uploading, and electronic sharing of any part of this book without the permission of
the publisher is unlawful piracy and theft of the author's intellectual property. If you
would like to use material from the book (other than for review purposes), prior written
permission must be obtained by contacting the publisher at permissions@hbgusa.com.
Thank you for your support of the author's rights.

All Scriptures are taken from the *Holy Bible, New International Version*®. Copyright © 1973,
1979, 1984, Biblica. Used by permission of Zondervan. All rights reserved.

Photography by Joe Alblas and Casey Crawford

Cover and interior design: Koechel Peterson & Associates, Inc., Minneapolis, Minnesota.

FaithWords
Hachette Book Group
237 Park Avenue
New York, NY 10017
www.faithwords.com

Printed in the United States of America

WOR

First Edition: February 2014

10 9 8 7 6 5 4 3 2 1

FaithWords is a division of Hachette Book Group, Inc.

The FaithWords name and logo are trademarks of Hachette Book Group, Inc.

The Hachette Speakers Bureau provides a wide range of authors for speaking events.
To find out more, go to www.hachettespeakersbureau.com or call (866) 376-6591.

The publisher is not responsible for websites (or their content) that are not
owned by the publisher.

LCCN: 2013951550

ISBN: 978-1-4555-4587-2

"Change the world."

This was the grand mission that Jesus had
declared to the Galilean fisherman named
Peter when he called him to leave his nets
and follow and become a fisher of men.
In the three years of discipleship that followed,
Peter had seen that word fulfilled in people's
lives over and over again.

Word of Jesus' miracles—changing water to wine, healing the sick and paralyzed, freeing those who are possessed by demons, feeding crowds of thousands—spread quickly throughout Galilee. When he entered a town with his disciples, hundreds flocked to his side, shuffling for position in the moving tide of humanity that engulfed him. The phenomenon had grown with every mile and every footstep, every village and town.

Jesus had taught his disciples during their daily walks from city to city. His simple, poetic words were delivered casually and gently. Jesus preferred to explain a difficult concept over time, never talking down to his followers, patiently letting the words soak in until they finally understood them fully.

But Jesus didn't just instruct his disciples. The religious revolution he started was a grassroots movement: he preached on dirt roads, in fields and villages, to farmers and fishermen and all manner of travelers. He stopped often, standing on a hillside or by a lake, to address the thousands who flocked to hear him, declaring his new vision for the relationship between God and man. To the people, Jesus' words feel like a spiritual rebirth. His goal is to liberate these oppressed people, who suffer so dearly under the Romans. But Jesus has no plan to form an army to save the Israelites from Rome. His purpose is to free them from something far more dire: sin.

Jesus also had no intention of waging a battle for religious power. But as his ministry grew, he found himself wading into a complex quagmire of political and religious movements. God, Rome, and religion are intertwined throughout Israel, and the two most powerful religious groups, the Pharisees and the Sadducees, have united in their view that Jesus endangers their relationship with Rome and their way of life. The most powerfully religious in Israel make up the Sanhedrin. This council is the supreme court for all Jewish disputes and is led by a high priest appointed by Rome. The general consensus of the Sanhedrin is that Jesus must be stopped at any cost.

must be stopped

IT IS THE WEEK BEFORE PASSOVER, the holy day that marks the time in Jewish history when its people were spared from death and led out of slavery from Egypt. Ironically, they celebrate their freedom from past oppressors while suffering under the yoke of new pagan masters— the Romans, and specifically the Roman prefect to Judea, Pontius Pilate. The servitude seems to never end.

Even as all of Israel prepares to celebrate this most important and sacred occasion, one select group of pilgrims is making their way to Jerusalem. Jesus walks at the front of the single-file line, leading his disciples and Mary Magdalene, whom Jesus had delivered from demons.

They are not alone on the dusty road leading into the city. Thousands of people walk dutifully in from the countryside and desert—the elderly, men pushing handcarts, women leading the family donkeys. Now and again the crowd parts to let Roman soldiers through, knowing that to obstruct their path might lead to a sudden but common act of brutality.

For Jesus, Passover week is off to a rousing start. Having heard about Jesus for years, the people of Jerusalem now celebrate his entry into their city. He rides a donkey, which is unusual for a man who walks everywhere, but it is the traditional way a king would come to visit his subjects if he came in peace. Hundreds of people line his path, throwing palm branches onto the ground to carpet the road. They chant "Hosanna," which means "save us," for even more than a spiritual teacher, these people hope that Jesus is the new King of the Jews who will save them from the Romans. "Hosanna," they chant over and over. The roar is deafening, and Jesus gladly acknowledges them all. The disciples walk on either side of him, somewhat dazzled by the excitement. This first big test of Jesus' popularity since he left Galilee is a success far beyond any expectation.

It is also audacious. Jesus has chosen to make his entry into Jerusalem on the donkey because Scripture foretells that the King of the Jews will enter Jerusalem as a humble man riding on a donkey. The symbolism is not lost on the crowd, who know their Scripture well.

"It is written!" they cry in the midst of their hosannas, clapping and chanting and waving palm fronds as a sign of fealty. Their faces are alight with hope as they imagine the day when they will throw off the Roman yoke. This is the One, the man who will bring a new peaceful age, free from poverty and suffering.

It is written.

It is written.

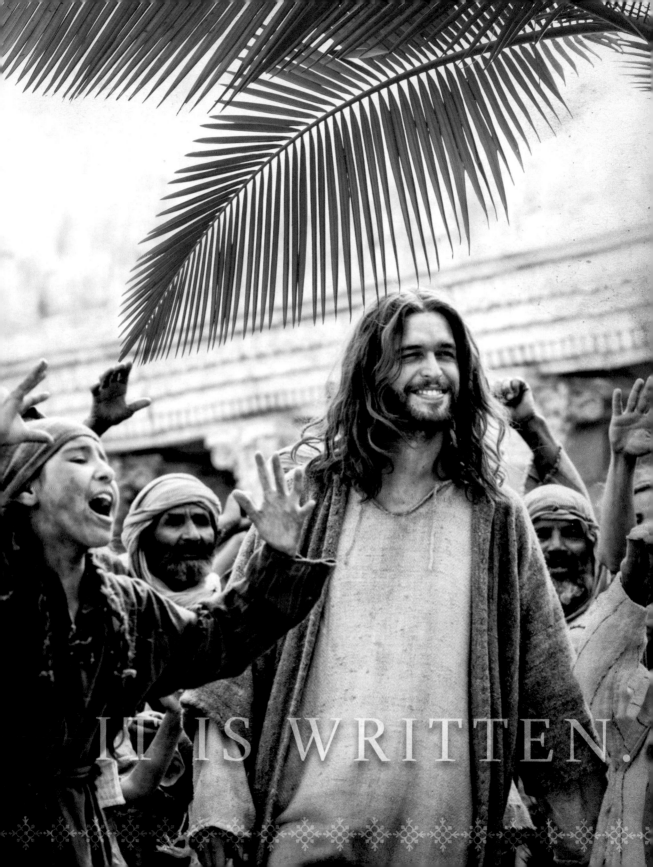

IT IS WRITTEN.

"A DONKEY?" Caiaphas, the leader of the San-hedrin, fumes when his servant Malchus tells him of Jesus' mode of transportation.

The elders of the Temple stand with him, shaking their heads. Jesus' arrival represents a direct challenge to their authority. Claims that Jesus is the Messiah have outraged and incensed the Sanhedrin, the Sadducees, and the Pharisees. Only they can anoint the new Messiah, and this carpenter from Nazareth is clearly not such a man.

"See your king comes to you," Caiaphas sarcastically quotes from Scripture. "Triumphant and victorious, humble and riding on a donkey."

The elders are silent.

"And where is he headed?" Caiaphas asks the servant.

"The Temple."

"The Temple!"

One of the elders named Nicodemus quotes another verse: "To lead his people to victory and throw out the oppressors."

"How are the crowds responding?" Caiaphas demands of the servant.

Malchus had hoped to impress the Sanhedrin by racing to tell them of Jesus' whereabouts. Yet it seems that every word that comes from his mouth is just another variation of bad news, so he says nothing.

Caiaphas knows precisely what that means. He paces animatedly, clearly worried. "Have the Romans made a move against him yet?"

Malchus shakes his head.

"Not yet," says a concerned Caiaphas. "We don't need Pilate feeling threatened or intervening, particularly during Passover. If we have a repeat of those executions, there's no telling what kind of anarchy will erupt."

Nicodemus agrees. "Last time Pilate felt threatened, hundreds of Jews were killed," he says, stating what everyone in the room was thinking.

Caiaphas nods to Nicodemus. "Go with Malchus. If Jesus enters the Temple, you watch him. I want to know every move he makes."

JESUS URGES HIS DONKEY on toward the Temple's outer wall. Peter, John, and the other disciples quicken their pace to keep up. The crowd continues chanting as they part to let Jesus through. The apostles grow anxious as they realize that these people are expecting amazing things from Jesus—not just miracles, but a complete revitalization of Israel.

"It is written," voices cry out from the crowd, "he will be called 'Wonderful Counselor, Mighty God, Everlasting Father, Prince of Peace.'"

Jesus would normally shy away from such profound benedictions. Instead, much to the apostles' shock, he welcomes them and is riding straight for the heart of his people's national identity: the Temple of Jerusalem. This can mean just one thing: the situation is about to explode. John scans the crowd nervously and notes that spies and messengers, whose faces are bereft of the joy possessed by so many others in the crowd, as well as Roman soldiers, are monitoring their actions.

At last Jesus reaches the Temple, dismounts from the donkey, and begins climbing the staircase to the Temple's outer gate. The great palace of worship is filled with Temple officials and moneychangers. The mood is tense, a stark contrast to the reception Jesus enjoyed as he entered the city. The disciples are concerned that things could get out of hand. This is a time to remain completely calm, not upsetting anyone or inviting trouble.

Jesus reaches the outer court of the great Jerusalem Temple complex—the Court of the Gentiles, as it is known. He walks ahead of the disciples with a purpose to his every footfall and a determination in his eyes.

Judas is frightened. "I don't like the looks of this," he says in a hushed voice. His fascination with being a disciple has been wearing thin lately, and he's not as eager as the others to lay down their lives for Jesus.

All around them, the great court is filled with activity. Lambs, doves, and goats are for sale, and their sounds and smells add to the human cacophony. There is the familiar clink of coins being counted and changing hands. The climax of Passover is a ritual animal sacrifice. Poor pilgrims traveling into Jerusalem from all over Israel must part with their hard-earned money to buy the animals. But their coins bear images of Roman emperors or Greek gods that are thought to be idolatrous by the Temple priests. So pilgrims must change all coins into Temple currency. A portion of the proceeds from the exchange goes to the Temple authorities, part goes to the Romans in taxes, and the rest is pocketed by the corrupt moneychangers who charge the pilgrims more than the law allows for making the currency exchange.

Jesus stops and studies all that is going on around him. His face and eyes are the picture of sadness. He sees more than just animals and moneychangers: an old man being shooed away by an angry moneychanger, a poor family trying to buy a lamb but having only enough for doves, and a frail old woman being jostled. The commotion makes it impossible for anyone to engage in devout prayer. Jesus' face clouds with anger and resentment, then he walks calmly toward the moneychangers' stall. Coins are piled on the tables. Their hands are dirty from counting money. They banter with one another. Jesus grabs the table edge with two hands and flips it over. Then he goes on to the next table and does the same. All heads in the Temple court turn to the sound of spilling coins, and onlookers immediately race to scoop up the fallen money.

"What are you doing?" shrieks one moneychanger.

Judas sees a band of Roman soldiers lining up like riot police near the entrance to the Temple complex. "Jesus! Please!" he pleads. He doesn't have the stomach for Jesus' brand of revolution. He fears he will be thrown into prison along with Jesus and all the disciples.

But Jesus doesn't listen to Judas or anyone else. Another table gets flipped.

"Why?" shouts one vendor, angry about all his earnings scattered about the Temple floor. "Why have you done this?"

"Is it not written?" Jesus declares in a booming voice that echoes throughout the chamber. "My house shall be called a house of prayer. But you have turned it into a den of thieves."

Nicodemus from the Sanhedrin steps forward. "Who are you to tell us this? How dare you. We interpret God's law—not you."

"You're more like snakes than teachers of the law," Jesus replies in a heated tone.

Nicodemus is beyond shocked. "Wait! You can't say that! We uphold the law. We serve God."

"No," Jesus replies. "You pray lofty prayers and strut about the Temple, impressed by your own piety. But you are merely hypocrites."

Nicodemus is stunned. No one speaks to men of his rank in this manner.

Jesus reaches out and gently lifts the fine material of Nicodemus's robe, rubbing the fine threads between his fingers. "It is much harder for a rich person to enter the Kingdom of God than it is for a camel to go through the eye of a needle," Jesus tells him, letting go of the robe.

Nicodemus looks about uneasily, feeling trapped. The pilgrim crowd is definitely on Jesus' side. At the far end of the chamber, he sees the Roman soldiers prepared to move in if the situation escalates. Such an intervention would further discredit the Temple elders and Sanhedrin, so Nicodemus says nothing as Jesus walks away.

Jesus' actions in the Temple confirm Caiaphas's worst fears. He and a handful of elders have been watching the action from a balcony high above the Temple floor. The chant of the crowd still vibrates throughout the great chamber long after Jesus has left. The people have been energized by Jesus, which makes the elders very nervous.

"This is outrageous!" fumes Caiaphas, who normally prides himself on his stoic behavior, preferring to appear unruffled and untroubled at all times.

A slightly breathless Nicodemus comes up the steps and joins them.

"You weren't much help," says Caiaphas.

"He's clever," Nicodemus counters. "The crowd worships him. There's something unusual about him that is easy for people to draw near."

"There's absolutely nothing unusual about him," Caiaphas snaps, "except for his ability to create havoc!"

Caiaphas turns back to view the scene, noticing that one of Jesus' disciples has approached his servant Malchus. There is an exchange between them. At first Caiaphas fears that their words will be angry, but whatever this particular disciple is saying surprises Malchus. The two clearly reach an agreement and then part ways. As the disciple hurries to catch up with Jesus, Malchus cranes his head upward to where Caiaphas stands. The look on his face is all Caiaphas needs to see. Judas will betray Jesus.

As Jesus leaves the Temple, the disciples, a crowd of excited new followers, and a few Jewish elders who want to know more about Jesus' teachings follow him. Malchus trails far behind as Caiaphas's spy.

Jesus leads this unlikely procession of old friends, new friends, elders, and a spy down the Temple steps, then suddenly stops, turns, and faces them. "Do you see this great building?" he asks them. "I tell you that not one stone of this place will be left standing."

A Jewish elder heard Jesus' words and asks, "Who are you to say these things?"

Jesus continues speaking to his disciples: "Destroy this Temple, and I will build it again in three days."

"But it took forty-six years to build!" replies the shocked elder. "How is this possible?"

Jesus doesn't answer him. He abruptly turns and continues on his way, leaving his disciples scratching their heads as to what Jesus meant.

"What does he mean?" asks Thomas, the disciple who is constantly doubtful. "Destroy the Temple? I don't get it."

John has a gift for vision and insight that is unparalleled among the disciples. "He's saying that we don't need a stone Temple to worship in. *He* will be our access to God."

"Really?" Thomas questions him, once again showing his unerring ability to question every fact.

With that, John and Thomas hurry to catch up with Jesus.

PONTIUS PILATE'S JERUSALEM RESIDENCE is far more sumptuous than his home in Caesarea, which is a good thing, because he rarely feels comfortable venturing outside when he's in Jerusalem. The city is totally Jewish, which is in stark contrast to the Roman design and Roman population of Caesarea. He feels like a complete foreigner when in Jerusalem, living in a small world with a completely different set of rules and way of life.

As Pilate and his wife, Claudia, take lunch on the veranda, Antonius, his top military commander, enters and salutes. News of Jesus' confrontation with the moneychangers spread through Jerusalem in a matter of minutes, but it's only now that Pilate is about to hear of Jesus for the first time.

"We are eating!" barks Pilate.

"So sorry to bother you, sir. But a Jew has been causing trouble in the Temple."

"You interrupt our meal for that?"

"Sir, he attacked the moneychangers and said he will destroy the Temple."

Pilate laughs. It is the first time Antonius has ever seen Pilate laugh, and the sight makes him uncomfortable.

"He has a very large number of supporters," he adds.

Pilate's smile disappears. "What's his name?" he asks.

"They call him Jesus of Nazareth."

This catches Claudia's attention. "My servants talk about him," she says.

Pilate looks at her quizzically and then back to Antonius. He has made up his mind. "This Jesus is Caiaphas's business, not mine. But keep your eye on these crowds following him. If they get out of hand, I will shut down the Temple, festival or no festival."

CAIAPHAS AND THE HIGH PRIESTS are gathered, discussing the situation with his servant Malchus and his handpicked group of elders, including Nicodemus.

"He said what?" asks an incredulous Caiaphas.

Malchus is the first to reply: "That he would destroy the Temple."

"I am shocked!" Caiaphas blurts out, steadying himself against the shock waves pounding his body. This is far worse than he thought. "He claims to be a man of God, and then says he plans to destroy the House of our Lord? We must act very fast, but with care. If we arrest him openly, his supporters will riot, and then Pontius Pilate will crack down." Caiaphas pauses, thinking through a new plan. "We must arrest him quietly at night . . . before Passover. Malchus, what was the name of that friend of his?"

"Judas."

"Yes, Judas. Bring him here. Discreetly."

JESUS AND HIS DISCIPLES camp on the hillside of the Mount of Olives, surrounded by pilgrims who have made their way to Jerusalem for the Holy Day. Smoke from the many campfires rises into the evening sky, and rows of tents cover the hill.

"Has anyone seen Judas?" Peter asks.

They all shake their heads. Jesus looks to Peter but doesn't offer an answer.

A figure steps out of the looming darkness and cautiously approaches Jesus. He wears a cloak that covers his Temple robes. When he pulls back his hood, the face of Nicodemus, a member of the Sanhedrin and a Pharisee, is revealed. He has come down under the cover of night to discover for himself what Jesus is about.

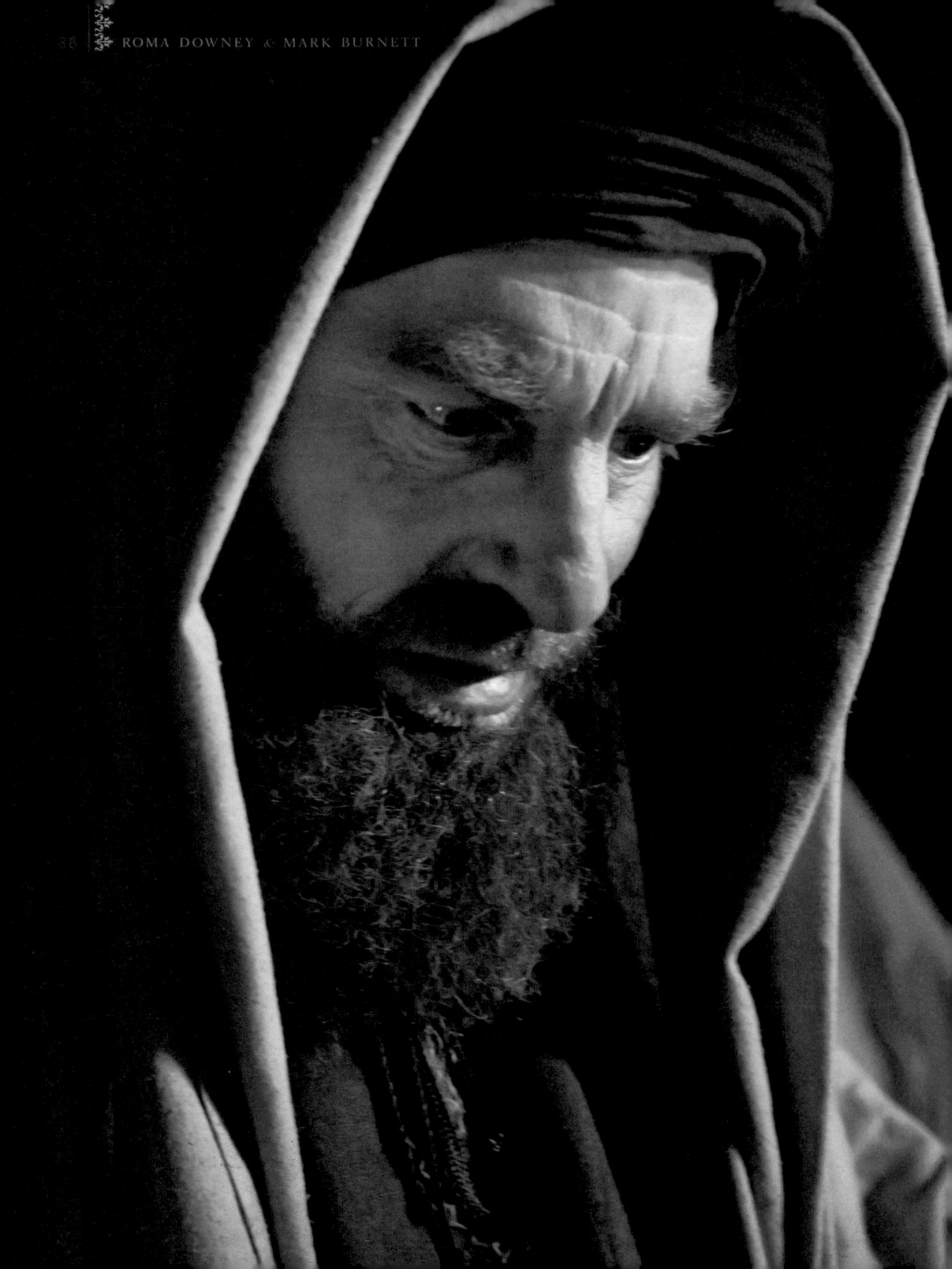

"What are you doing here?" Thomas demands. A man of Nicodemus's position would never normally associate with ordinary people.

Nicodemus appears tense, but then Jesus steps forward and kindly says, "Welcome," which puts Nicodemus at ease, and he joins Jesus by the fire.

With a full moon shining its light down through the olive grove, Nicodemus starts the conversation. "Rabbi, they say you can perform miracles—that you have seen the Kingdom of God."

"You, too, can see the Kingdom of God," Jesus assures him. "But you must be born again."

"Born again. Whatever do you mean? How is that possible? Surely we cannot enter our mother's womb a second time."

"You must be reborn—though not in the flesh, but of water and spirit. That which is born of flesh is flesh, and that which is born of the spirit is spirit."

A sudden wind blows Jesus' hair across his face and rustles the tree branches. Nicodemus looks up into the branches. When he looks back, Jesus is staring at him intently.

"The wind blows where it wishes," he tells Nicodemus. "You hear its sound but don't know where it comes from or where it goes. So it is when the Spirit enters you. Believe in me, Nicodemus, and you will have eternal life."

"Believe in you?"

"For God so loved the world that he gave his one and only Son, that whoever believes in him shall have eternal life."

Nicodemus is torn. *Could this be the Messiah? Or is this just another false messiah, a deluded individual claiming to be God?*

Jesus knows his thoughts. "Everyone who does evil hates the light for fear that their deeds will be exposed. But those who live by the truth come into the light."

Nicodemus feels a great peace wash over him. The moonlight shines brightly, and the breeze blows gently.

God so loved the world....

AT THE ENTRANCE to Caiaphas's palace, Judas removes his hood so the Temple guards will allow him to enter. He is led into Caiaphas's inner sanctum, where he immediately feels ill at ease as he is brought to Caiaphas.

"One cannot deny that he has followers," Caiaphas begins, "especially among the less-educated elements of our society. But Judas . . . you intrigue me. You don't seem to be one of them. Why follow this man?"

"I can't explain Jesus to you. He has power. It's hard to put into words. He says things . . . things that other people don't even think, let alone speak."

"Things like destroying the Temple?" Caiaphas reasons.

What's in it for me?

Judas is extremely uneasy. "Well, I suppose that if he was the Son of God—*if*—then he could truly destroy the Temple. But why would he abuse the House of God? Surely the true Messiah would seek to unify Israel, not divide it."

"Judas, your friend Jesus can't possibly know where all this will lead. If the Romans step in, the slaughter will be beyond belief. They have done it before and can do it again. It will be the end of our Temple— and possibly even our faith. Do you want that?"

Judas remains silent as the high priest continues his argument.

"It's important that you help," says Caiaphas. "Help him, Judas. Help your friend. Save him from himself while you still can."

"And if I do? What's in it for me?"

If Caiaphas had any doubts that Judas's initial approach was one of betrayal, those doubts immediately vanish. Caiaphas reaches over to a table, on which rests a small purse. He holds up the purse.

Judas swallows hard in his moment of choice. "I'll do it," he says. He grabs the bag, and the silver coins clink inside.

JESUS RETURNS TO THE TEMPLE the next day, performing miracles and preaching to the swelling crowds in Jerusalem. The people are liberated and energized by his words and use the term *Messiah* almost casually, as if it is an acknowledged fact that Jesus is Lord. The groundswell of popular support, particularly during Passover, terrifies the high priests and the Temple guards. At all costs, they must avoid a riot. They know what Pilate would do, for this would be viewed as a revolution. But the religious authorities cannot stop Jesus. He's too beloved, too charismatic, and too authentic for them to make a move against him.

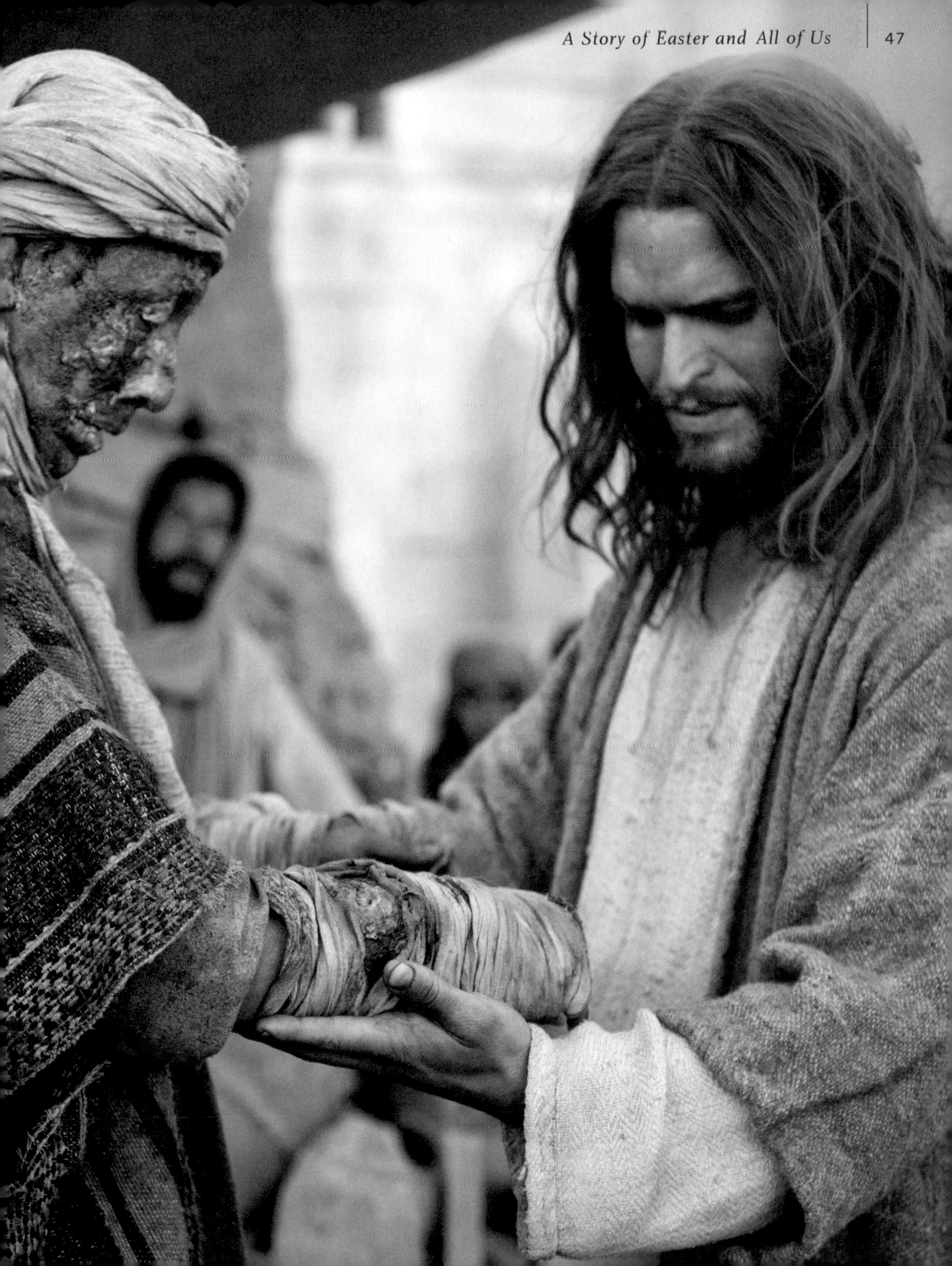

The same cannot be said for Pontius Pilate. The fervor of the crowds at the Temple is unlike anything he's ever seen, and he's sure that the situation is about to explode into full-scale rebellion against Rome. He calls Caiaphas to his palace and makes it all quite clear: "Stop the disturbances or the Temple will be shut down. There will be no Passover." The rage with which Pilate delivers the words is a reminder that he is more than just a random administrator sent by Rome to govern the Jews. *Pilate is the law in Israel.* Caiaphas and the priests owe their power to him, and him alone.

Caiaphas heads straight to his priests, then addresses the subject that is on all their minds. "We can't wait any longer. It's almost Passover. We must arrest this troublemaker—this false messiah—tonight."

"And how do we know he is false?" asks Nicodemus, which turns the room to stone silence.

Caiaphas resists the urge to berate Nicodemus in front of the others. "Has he fulfilled any of the signs of a true messiah, as it is written in our laws?" he asks coolly.

Nicodemus remains quiet. It is dangerous to argue with Caiaphas.

"He must be tried by our laws," Caiaphas demands. "Either we eliminate this one man, or the Romans will step in and destroy everything we have worked our entire lives for."

Nicodemus can't believe his ears. "Eliminate? Are you talking about executing this man?"

"What is the life of one deluded peasant when our people's lives are at stake?"

ON THE OTHER SIDE OF JERUSALEM, the streets are calm and the night air cool as Peter and Judas approach a small house and knock on the door.

"What does he want us for?" asks Judas.

"He wants us to take supper," Peter tells him.

"To eat together? Before Passover? That's strange."

The door opens. Mary Magdalene warmly welcomes them inside. "Everyone's upstairs," she tells them, motioning up with one arm. Mary remains downstairs as the disciples climb the stairs and enter a small room. A single long, low dining table fills the space. There is a place for each of the twelve disciples to sit.

The unleavened bread in front of them is hot from the oven, and its fresh-baked smell fills the room. The group prays together, asking that God bless their meal and their fellowship, and then the disciples begin to relax, reclining on cushions and tearing off pieces of bread.

But before they can eat, Jesus says calmly, "This will be our last meal together."

They all look at Jesus, stunned by the news.

"What about Passover?" Judas asks a little too quickly.

"I will be dead before Passover," Jesus replies.

Stunned silence follows until Peter finally demands, "What do you mean?"

Jesus doesn't answer, but John leans forward and whispers in Peter's ear. "Remember the discussion on the road to Jerusalem, where he prophesied that he would be betrayed, arrested, and condemned to death?"

Peter remembers. The thought fills him with dread. He has given up everything to follow Jesus, and he has been as loyal as any man can be. The thought that Jesus might die crushes Peter's spirit and pierces his heart.

"Don't worry," Jesus commands them. "Trust in God. Trust in me, also. You already know the way to where I am going."

Thomas is close to tears. "We don't know where you are going. How can we know the way?"

"But Thomas, you know that I am the way, the truth, and the life." Then Jesus makes it even more confusing. He tears off a piece of bread and hands it to John. "This is my body," he tells them all. "Take of it and eat."

John has tears streaming down his cheeks, for he understands. He opens his mouth, and Jesus places a morsel of the bread on his tongue. Then Jesus raises a cup of wine. "This is my blood. I will shed my blood so that your sins may be forgiven."

Bread and wine pass from hand to hand around the room. "Remember me by doing this. Soon I will go to be with the Father, but when you eat my bread and drink from my cup, you proclaim my glory, and I am with you always.

"But now I must tell you," Jesus continues, "one of you will betray me."

The wine is passed to Judas. He struggles to keep his composure; his eyes are riveted on Jesus.

"Who is it?" asks John. "Which one of us would do such a thing?"

Jesus tears off a piece of bread and passes it. "Whoever eats this will betray me."

All the disciples stare, transfixed, as the piece of bread is passed to Judas.

"It's not me," Judas protests, holding the bread in his hand but not eating. "I would never betray you, Lord."

Jesus' eyes stay fixed on Judas. Looking straight back at him, Judas takes the bread, eats it, and shudders.

The disciples all stare at him with a look of pure horror.

"Do it quickly," Jesus commands Judas.

Terrified, Judas scrambles to his feet and makes for the door. A disgusted Peter chases after him, not sure whether he will beat Judas to within an inch of his life or merely follow to make sure that Judas does not carry out this betrayal.

But Jesus calls out, "Peter, leave him! You will all fall away; even you, Peter."

"Never, Lord! I am loyal. I would never betray you."

"Peter," Jesus tells him, "before the cock crows at dawn, you will have denied knowing me three times."

Before Peter can protest, Jesus rises to his feet and says, "Come. Let us all leave."

CAIAPHAS STANDS TALL in his palace before Nicodemus. The high priest is calm and deliberate, while Nicodemus is deeply troubled by what is about to happen.

"Judas is bringing him to us before dawn," says Caiaphas.

"But the law does not allow it," insists Nicodemus. "A trial must be held in daylight!"

"And does our law allow riots? Does our law invite Romans to spill Jewish blood? You were there. You heard what Pilate said."

Judas bursts into the room.

"Where is he?" Caiaphas asks.

"I don't know," Judas replies, "but I know where he is going."

Caiaphas points to Malchus. "Lead my servant to him."

THE GARDEN OF GETHSEMANE is deserted, save for Jesus and his disciples. Jesus knows the time to leave his disciples and this world is fast approaching. He has spent the last hour in fervent prayer, but if the disciples are anxious about Jesus, they have an odd way of showing it—curled up on the ground, fast asleep.

"The spirit is willing, but the body is weak. Wake up," Jesus demands after observing them for a moment. He needs them to bear witness. "Stay awake. The hour is at hand."

Peter has tucked a long dagger into his belt. He double-checks to make sure it is there, making quiet plans to put it to good use should anyone attack Jesus.

Jesus leaves them, walking slowly back up the hill, once again to be alone with his Father. He knows Judas is almost here, leading a group of men who will arrest him by force. To endure what is about to take place, Jesus needs strength. As he arrives atop the hill, he immediately falls to his knees in prayer, presses his forehead into the dusty ground, clasps his hands together, and prays: "Father, if you are willing, take this cup from me. Your will not mine be done." Sweat falls from his brow as if it was great drops of blood pooling in the dirt. He knows he will die a human death and after three days, his body—the temple—will be raised from the dead, so that all humankind can be saved from the penalty of death. Jesus pleads for God to spare him the suffering and death, a form of temptation similar to when Satan tempted him in the desert three years ago. Indeed, Satan now lurks in the garden, watching Jesus cling to the hope that his life might be spared.

Jesus hears the sound of an approaching mob. Their torches light the base of the hill, and their manic voices cut through the night. Jesus' head is still bowed, as he now prays for the strength to carry out God's plan. Sweat continues to fall. Now that God's will is confirmed, resolve washes over him—not peace, for what he is about to endure cannot bring the gentle calm of peace, just resolve. "Your will, Father, is mine."

Jesus rises from his knees and stands alone in the grove of olive trees. His disciples suddenly burst over the rise and surround him protectively. A line of torches looms in the darkness, marching steadily toward them. "The time has come," Jesus says to everyone and no one.

Judas steps forth and kneels down behind Jesus, as if in prayer. Then he leans in and kisses Jesus on the cheek.

Jesus asks him, "Judas, you betray the Son of Man with a kiss?"

Infuriated, Peter draws his dagger and races toward Judas. Peter stabs at him, but misses. Malchus intervenes with the Temple guard, and Peter swipes the knife, severing Malchus's ear. "Run, Jesus," Peter yells. "Run while you can!"

Malchus spins away in pain, blood gushing down the side of his face. His severed ear falls to the ground as a circle of torches surround Jesus and the disciples. Jesus calmly lifts Malchus's ear from the ground and reaches for his bloody head. Malchus flinches, as if Jesus means to hit him. He is caught off guard when Jesus defies his defensive stance and gently touches his wound. When Jesus pulls his hand away, Malchus is stunned and confused that the few moments of indescribable pain are like a momentary dream. His ear is healed.

"Take him away!" a guard shouts as Malchus stands stunned, fingering his ear.

"Jesus!" moans Peter.

"It is my Father's will, Peter. It must happen this way."

Horrified, Peter watches as Jesus is shoved forward, grasped on both arms by strong men and surrounded by a half-dozen others, hooded, and dragged off.

The terrified disciples run off into the night, knowing their lives are on the line. Only Peter ignores John's pleas to come with him, and instead of running, he surreptitiously follows the line of torches down the hillside, desperate to see where Jesus is being taken.

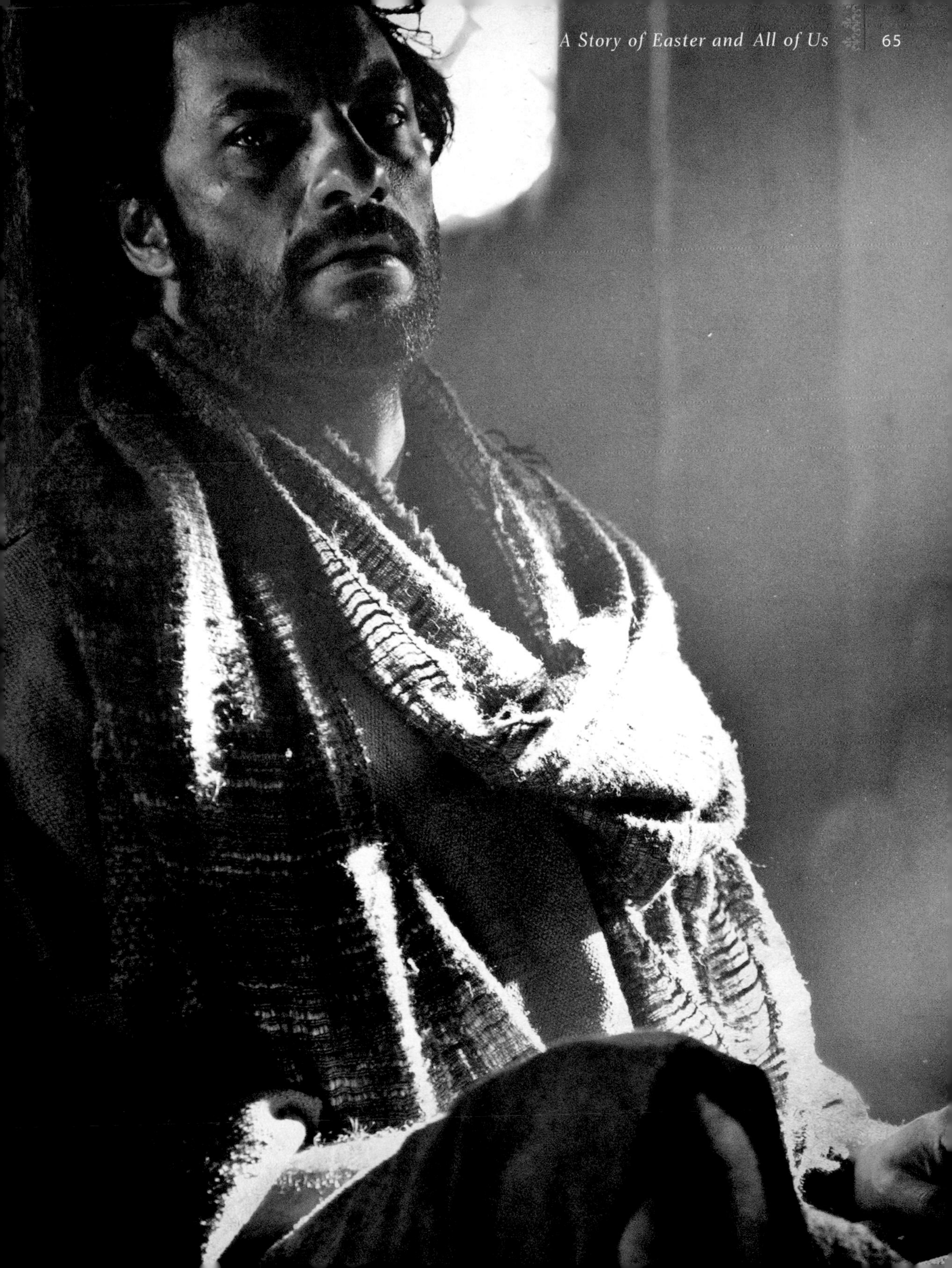

IT IS THE MIDDLE OF THE NIGHT in Jerusalem. Jesus has been beaten. Blood pours from his broken nose; his body is bruised, and his hands are bound. The Temple guards lead Jesus by a length of rope to Caiaphas and a hostile trial courtroom packed with the elders who comprise the Sanhedrin. Makers and keepers of Israel's religious laws, whatever these men decide is binding. The sun is about to rise.

"Brothers," Caiaphas begins, "thank you for coming at this hour. I wouldn't ask if this was not such a serious matter." Then he waves his hand and cries with mock reverence, "The one and only Jesus of Nazareth!"

Jesus does not look up or speak.

Jesus does not speak

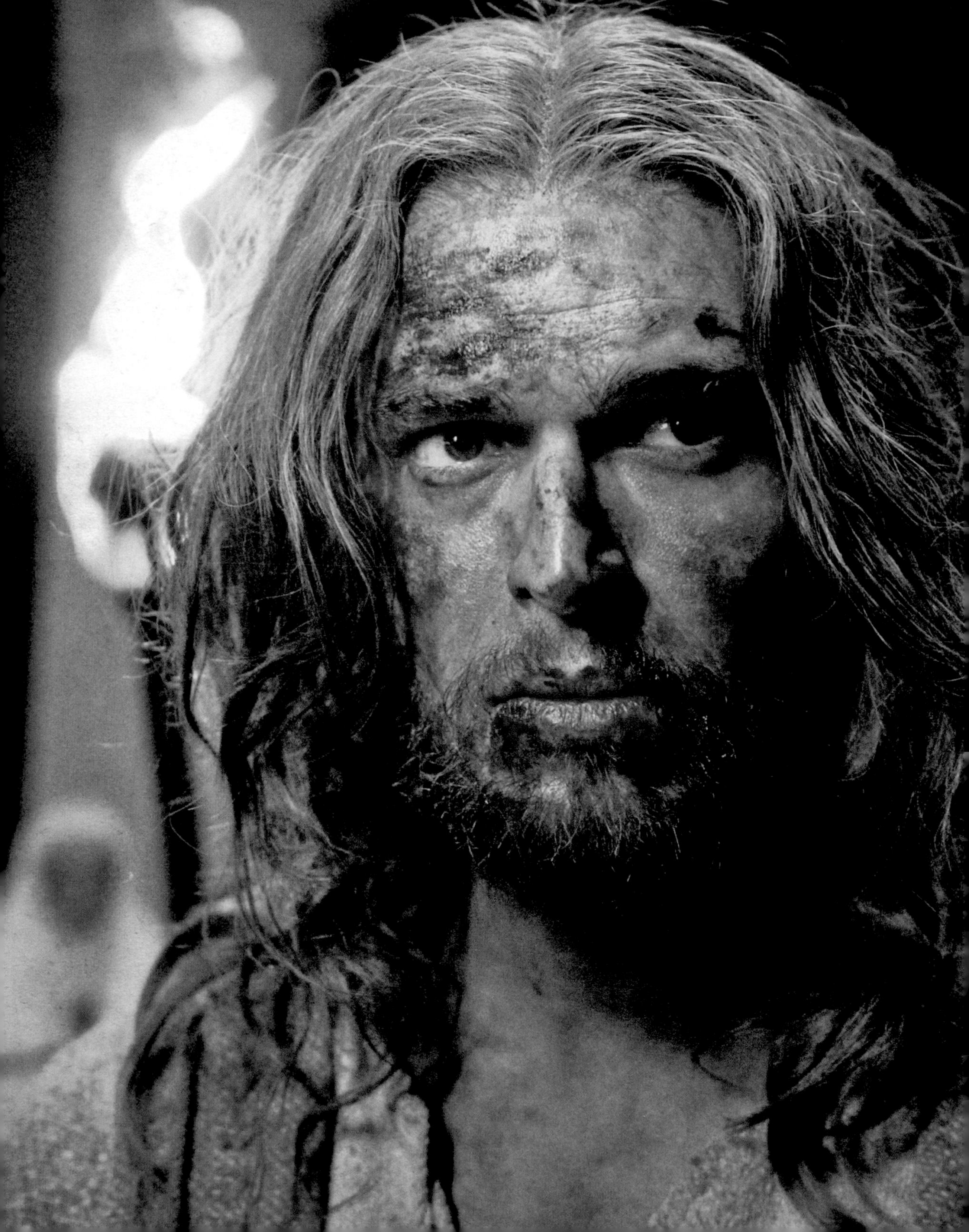

"Jesus of Nazareth," Caiaphas intones solemnly, "you are suspected of blasphemy. Now let us hear from our witnesses." Caiaphas beckons the first witness.

"In the Temple," says the man who steps forward, clearly intimidated, "he healed a lame woman in the Temple."

Nicodemus can't bear to look at Jesus. It's clear that the trial is going to be a charade. A second witness is asked to speak.

"He said he would destroy the Temple!"

"I heard him say that, too," chimes in a Temple elder.

Caiaphas points his finger at Jesus. "You would destroy the Temple! How dare you! That is rebellion against the Lord our God. Tell me, how do you answer these accusations?"

Jesus is silent. Nicodemus stares hard at him, willing him to speak up. But Jesus remains impassive. The outcome is already decided. Jesus gathers his strength for the ordeal that is soon to come.

"The witnesses' evidence is clear and unequivocal. My brothers, we have faced false prophets in the past, and we will face false prophets in the future. But I doubt we will face one as false as this!"

The room fills with murmurs of agreement.

A new voice cries out, that of an elder named Joseph of Arimathea. "A prophet brings us new words from God, does he not? If every new voice is crushed, how will we ever know a prophet when we hear one?"

Caiaphas is thrown off and chooses to deflect the question. "You are right, Joseph. How will we? We must listen and then judge. So I invite this man—this 'prophet'—to speak." He turns to Jesus. "Are you the Christ, the Son of God?"

Jesus slowly raises his head. His body stiffens, and he stands tall. He looks Caiaphas directly in the eye. "I am, and you will see the Son of Man sitting at the right hand of God and coming on the clouds of heaven."

"Impostor!" Caiaphas cries, ripping his robe open to seek forgiveness from God for hearing such words. "Blasphemer! We must vote, and we must vote now!"

Joseph of Arimathea and Nicodemus shake their heads at the sham, feeling helpless to stop it.

"The sentence is death!" Caiaphas cries out before a vote is taken.

"This is wrong!" yells Joseph. "This verdict brings shame on this council!"

Caiaphas ignores him.

THE DOORS OF CAIAPHAS'S PALACE swing open. Peter is standing just outside as Jesus is dragged out. Throughout the night, his own life has been in jeopardy as he has waited to hear what has happened to Jesus, hoping somehow he can help.

Others have come to stand outside Caiaphas's door, as word of Jesus' arrest has quickly traveled. This crowd of supporters is devastated by the sight of Jesus' battered body, with blood caked on his face and bruises around his eyes.

Malchus reads from a proclamation: "Let it be known that Jesus of Nazareth has been tried by the supreme court of Temple elders. He has been found guilty of blasphemy and threatening to destroy the Temple. The sentence is death."

The crowd gasps. Judas, who has remained outside all night, hurls the bag of silver at Malchus. "Take back your money!" he screams, distraught. This is not at all what he intended. The coins clatter to the cobblestones at the feet of Malchus.

A large guard approaches Peter. "You . . . I know you."

Peter doesn't scare easily. "I don't know what you're talking about."

"You know him," says the guard, grabbing at Peter. "You called him 'Rabbi.'"

"No," says Peter. "He has nothing to do with me."

"He's one of them!" a woman screams, pointing at Peter.

He spins around and confronts her. "I tell you, I don't know him!"

Peter sees Jesus being hauled away, and he is furious at his inability to help Jesus. The rooster crows, and Peter remembers Jesus' words that he would deny knowing his beloved friend and teacher before dawn. The rough gruff man sobs in agony.

"WHERE IS MY SON?" asks Mary. She stands over Peter. The crowd has dispersed, and she has found the sobbing fisherman lying alone in the gutter.

"They've condemned him."

Mary gasps in shock.

"They've taken him. I don't know where, but he's gone." Peter slowly rises to his feet, aided by John. "I told them I didn't know him!" Peter cries out, inconsolable. Then he breaks away and disappears down the street.

Mary sinks to the ground as the sun glints off the high walls of the Temple complex. Her mother's heart clearly understands that daybreak brings little hope. The disciples are broken and powerless against the authority of the high priest.

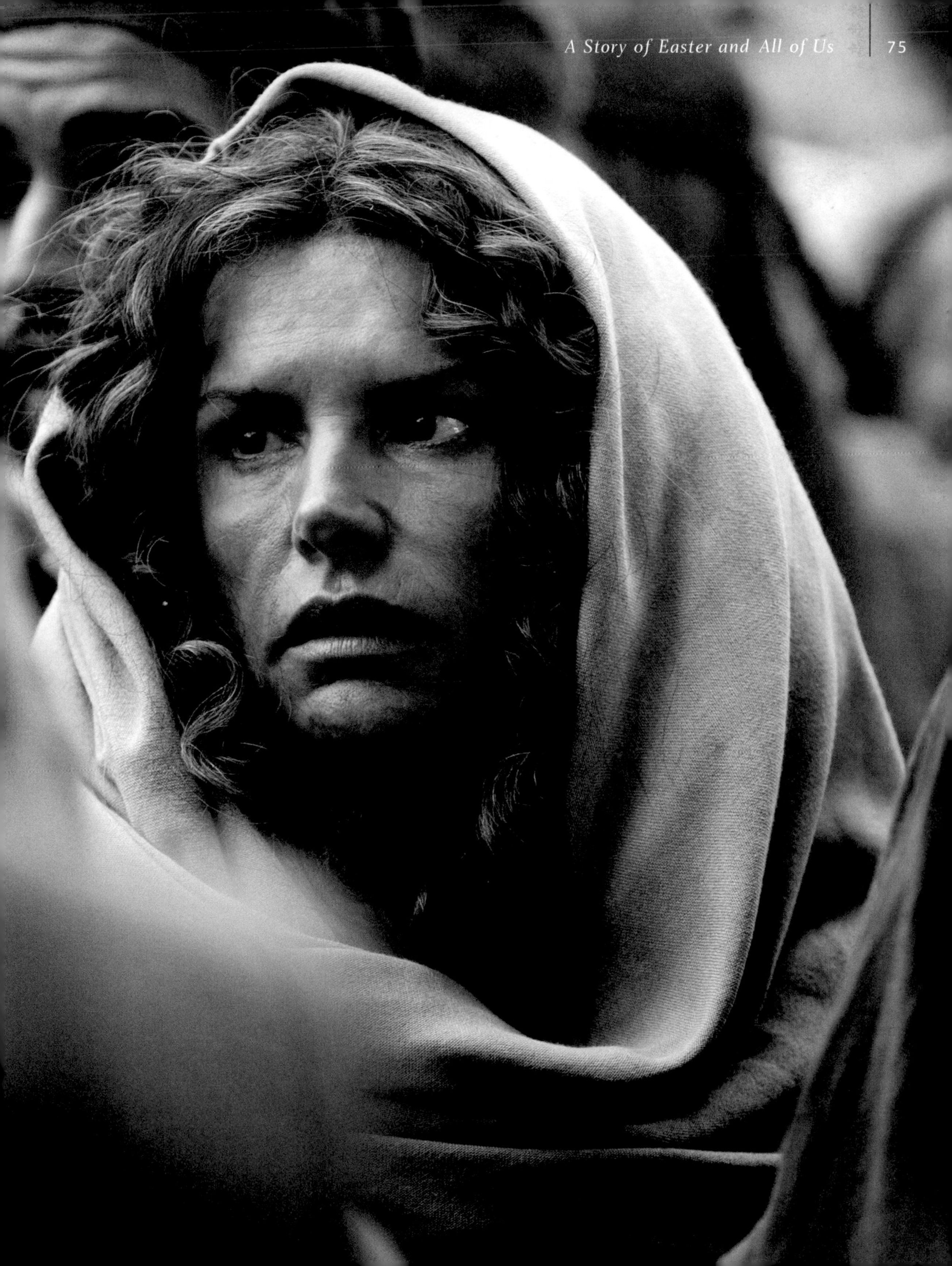

PILATE STANDS BEFORE A WASHBASIN in his residence. As he finishes washing his face, a servant hands him a towel. "Where's my wife?" asks Pilate. "She should be up by now."

Just then, the maidservant of Pilate's wife appears in the doorway. "Master, come quickly, please!"

Pilate follows her immediately down the empty corridor to his wife's room, where Claudia lies on the bed drenched in sweat and hyperventilating. He goes to comfort her.

"I saw a man," whispers Claudia, "in a dream."

Dreams are serious business to the Romans, portenders of the future that should never be ignored. "Tell me about this dream," says Pilate.

"I saw a man being beaten and killed—an innocent man . . . a holy man," she says, then adds, "a good man. It is a warning."

"And why is that?"

"Because in my dream, you killed this man."

THE BRANCHES of a giant ancient olive tree swing in the early morning breeze as Jerusalem greets the day. Its gnarled thick branches rise to a lofty height. Judas Iscariot slips the halter around his neck. The leather is rough against his skin. He then loops the other end of the halter around a thick branch and tugs on it to make sure the connection is taut. Taking one last look at Jerusalem, and hoping for God's mercy, Judas leaps.

Pilate is tending to governmental matters inside the Roman governor's residence when Caiaphas is announced.

"Prefect, we need your help," says Caiaphas. "We have convicted and sentenced a dangerous criminal to death."

"And . . . when is his execution?"

Caiaphas moves closer, spreading his hands as if in explanation. "We—the Sanhedrin—cannot. It's Passover, you see, and against our law." Caiaphas punctuates his tale by bowing his head deferentially.

"So do it after Passover," says Pilate, looking at him with distaste. "Surely the man can live a few more days."

"Normally, I would say yes. But this man is an urgent threat—not only to us, but also to Rome. He claims to be our king and is using that lie to whip my people into rebellion. This man could very well tear Jerusalem apart."

Pilate looks at Caiaphas, wondering how such a pompous individual became the leading voice in the Jewish religion. His patience with the man is at a breaking point. "I am quick to punish criminals, but only if they break the law. I need proof that this man has done so."

"He has broken the law, Prefect. I assure you," Caiaphas replies.

"You had better be right," snarls Pilate, fixing Caiaphas with a deadly gaze. "If you're wasting my time, you'll pay for this." He looks at his guards. "I'll see the prisoner."

A RAGGED BLOODSTAINED HOOD hangs over Jesus' head as he languishes in the cells located within Pilate's residence. This was once home to Herod the Great, who banished his own sons to these same cells and then put them to death. The same fate befell John the Baptist. Now Pilate will decide whether Jesus should face the same punishment.

The Roman governor enters, and a guard pulls off Jesus' hood. The Messiah slowly raises his eyes and looks directly at Pilate, who is unnerved, just as Caiaphas was unnerved by these same eyes.

"So," Pilate begins after a very long pause, "are you the King of the Jews?"

Silence.

"They say you claim to be King of the Jews."

"Is that what you think, or did others tell you this about me?" Jesus replies calmly.

Pilate takes a step back and momentarily averts his eyes. "Your own people say that," Pilate replies, regaining his composure. "So tell me: are you a king?"

"My kingdom is not of this world," answers Jesus. "If it was, my servants would fight my arrest."

"So you are a king?"

"You say rightly that I am a king. I was born to come into the world and testify to the truth; everyone who is of the truth hears my voice."

"Truth? What is truth?" demands Pilate.

Jesus says nothing. He smiles and looks up into the single shaft of light that penetrates the dark cell. It bathes his face. The enraged governor feels like slapping the insolent prisoner, but there is something unusual about this prisoner that stops him in his tracks. He looks at Jesus for what feels like an eternity, then turns and leaves.

Claudia greets him as he returns to his office. "Well?" she asks.

"They want him crucified," answers Pilate.

"You can't. I beseech you!"

"Why? This man is only a Jew. They say he wants to start a revolution."

"I tell you, my love, this is the man from my dreams. The man you killed. Please don't do this. His blood will be on your hands."

"And if I don't and there is a rebellion, how will I explain it to Rome? Caiaphas will surely blame me. Caesar has already warned me once and is not going to warn me again. I will be finished . . . *we'll* be finished."

Claudia places a hand on his shoulder, though she doesn't say a word, knowing that her husband often needs to focus his thoughts before taking action.

"Get me Caiaphas," Pilate says after a moment. "I have a plan."

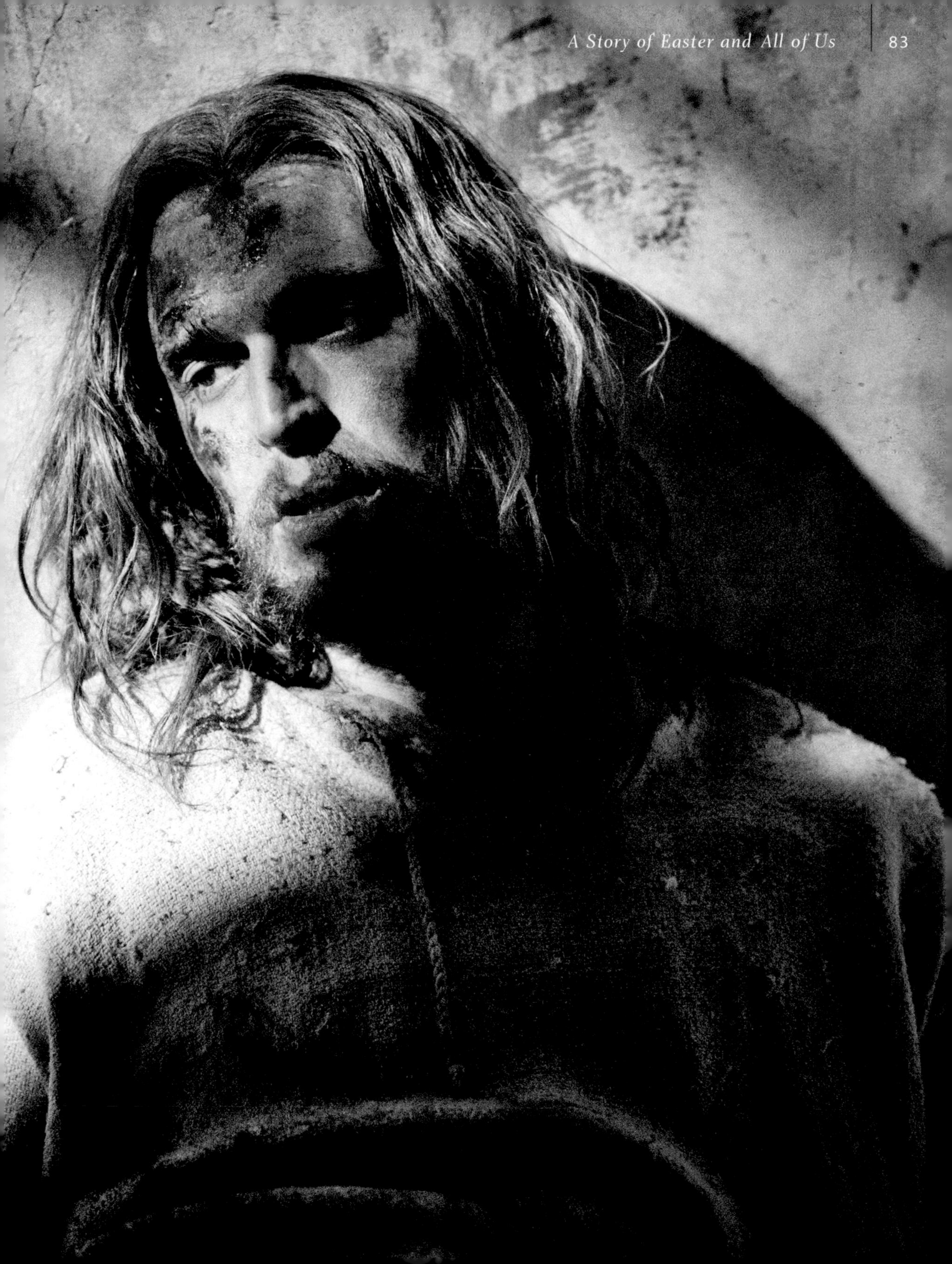

PILATE GREETS CAIAPHAS and the elders with thinly veiled contempt. "I have met your Jesus and concluded that he is guilty of nothing more than being deranged. That is not a crime in Rome."

"He's broken the law," Caiaphas protests.

"*Your* law," Pilate replies smoothly. "Not Caesar's." The governor stares hard at Caiaphas. "Teach this man some respect. Give him forty lashes and dump him outside the city walls. That is my decree."

"Nothing more? Prefect, I cannot be held responsible for what the people will do if you release a man who has broken our sacred laws. Especially on this day, when our eyes are on God."

"The people?" Pilate responds sarcastically, knowing his next move. Even as Caiaphas tries to take control, Pilate speaks first. "Caesar decrees that I can release a prisoner at Passover. I shall let 'the people' decide which of the prisoners in my jails shall be crucified and which shall be set free."

Caiaphas knows he's been tricked, but he's too stunned to speak.

"Send for the prisoner," Pilate orders.

A crowd is now gathered at the gate outside Pilate's residence, peering through a large steel grate into the empty courtyard, including Mary, Jesus' mother, Mary Magdalene, and John. Word has gone out that Jesus will be lashed. Many like to witness public brutality and revel in the carnival-like proceedings that accompany a good beating.

Two Roman soldiers drag Jesus into the courtyard. His face is crusted in blood, and his eyes are now swollen shut by a fresh round of beatings.

Mary, his mother, gasps.

Jesus is tied to the whipping post. His robes are ripped from his back, exposing the flesh. The soldiers now retrieve their whips. A single lash is an exercise in agony, sure to scar a man for life. Jesus is about to endure thirty-nine.

"They're going to kill him," Mary whispers to Mary Magdalene, her heart breaking.

The two soldiers stand ready to whip, one on each side of Jesus. They will each take turns. A third soldier enters the courtyard, carrying an abacus. It will be his job to make a careful tally of the blows and report back to Rome that precisely thirty-nine were inflicted.

Jesus looks across to his mother. Her pain is enormous, but his eyes lock with hers and she feels a strong connection with him. It is as if he is reassuring her and reminding her that this is how it must be.

The lashings begin. Jesus does not cry out, even as the crowd gasps at the severity of what they are witnessing. The harrowing punishment and ordeal Jesus is to endure has been preordained. Isaiah, the prophet, once wrote that there would come a Savior who "was pierced through for our transgressions. He was crushed for our iniquities. And by his scourging, we are healed."

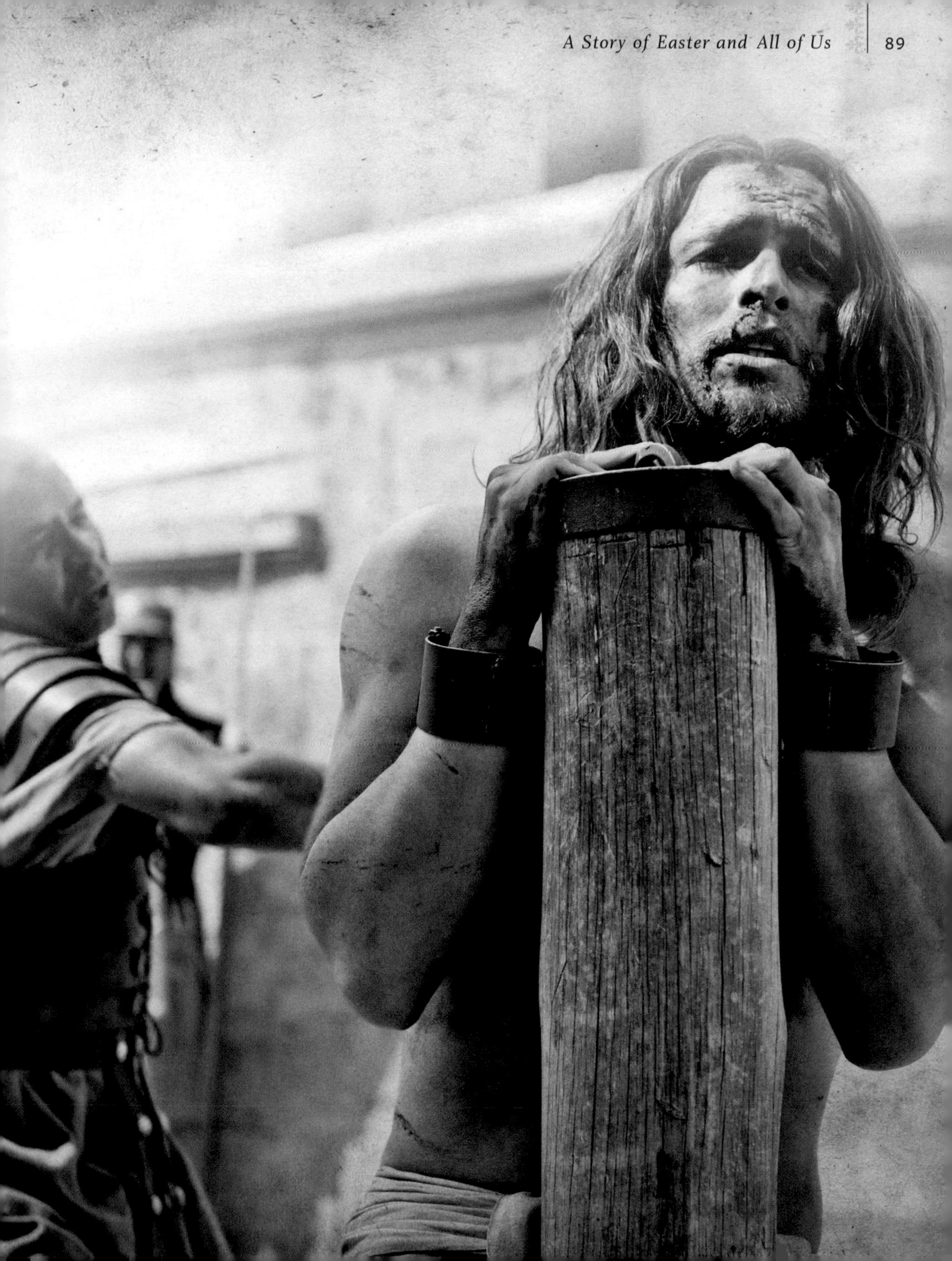

Finally, one last abacus bead slides from left to right. Thirty-nine lashes are in the books.

Jesus hangs on the pole, barely alive but definitely breathing. When his hands are untied, he does not slump to the ground but stands upright, beaten but unbroken.

Now he is taken back to the dungeon. The guards, never known to show kindness toward their prisoners, especially Jews, have been busy while he was away. To have this delusional prisoner in their midst claiming to be a king is the stuff of folly, and they can't wait to take advantage. One guard has woven a crown out of thorny branches. It is gruesome to behold, with long spikes sticking out at all angles. He presses it down hard on Jesus' skull, drawing blood as those sharp tips bite into bone. "King of the Jews!" the soldier exults, bowing deep in front of Jesus, then dancing a little jig.

One of the soldiers who beat Jesus wipes the blood from his hands and then drapes the crimson towel over Jesus' shoulders as if it were an ermine robe. The jailers find this hilarious.

PILATE ORDERS that the palace gates be opened. The crowds move in, not sure what is about to happen. They know Pilate is allowed to release one prisoner of their choice before Passover. They wonder who will be set free and assume Jesus is no longer a consideration, for he has paid his penalty and by law should have been released. So they wait patiently for their options.

Skillfully deflecting Caiaphas's demand that he crucify Jesus, Pilate is giving the final verdict to this mass of pilgrims. Caiaphas remains undeterred, however, and is ensuring that the pilgrims allowed into the courtyard will vote against Jesus. Malchus and the Temple guards stand at the gates, denying entry to anyone who supports the man from Nazareth.

Mary, John, and Mary Magdalene are among those kept away. They watch in disbelief as a mob of pro-Caiaphas sympathizers stand ready to determine Jesus' fate.

Pontius Pilate appears in an upstairs window, and the crowd silences to hear what he has to say. "Today," Pilate begins, "Passover begins. Caesar makes you a gesture of goodwill through the release of a prisoner chosen by you."

A bald-headed murderer is marched into the courtyard, followed by Jesus, still wearing his crown of thorns.

"You may choose between Barabbas, a murderer," Pilate declares, "and this teacher who claims to be your king."

Laughter and jeers spew forth from the crowd. Caiaphas, who now stands at Pilate's side, yells, "We have no king but Caesar!"

"Decide!" Pilate shouts to the crowd.

"Barabbas!" they roar back. "Free Barabbas!"

Outside the gates, Mary, John, and Mary Magdalene all shout in Jesus' defense, as do many around them. But their voices cannot be heard over the courtyard roar.

Pilate is mystified. He looks at Caiaphas and then back at the crowd, holding up a hand for silence. "You choose a murderer," he tells them with a shake of his head. "Do it," he orders his bewildered guards, who reluctantly unlock Barabbas's shackles.

"And this wretch!" Pilate yells to the crowd. "What shall I do with Jesus?"

"Crucify him! Crucify him!"

Pilate again silences the crowd. "How can you condemn this man and spare a murderer?"

"Crucify! Crucify! Crucify!"

"Very well," he declares. "Crucify him!"

Pilate reaches for a nearby bowl of water and washes his hands—a deliberate gesture, mirroring a custom of the Hebrews and Greeks, to show that he is not responsible. "I am innocent of this man's blood," he states, hoping to shift blame, though he knows Jesus is innocent and has the power to release him and simply disperse the mob. But instead of standing up for truth, he takes the easier route of political expediency. It is a dangerous time in Jerusalem, the home to more than a million Jews and less than a thousand Roman soldiers. Pilate cannot risk a tumult, as it would make its way back to Rome and Caesar.

Pilate dries his hands. This crucifixion is no longer his affair.

IT HAS BEEN JUST SIX DAYS since Jesus was welcomed into Jerusalem with shouts of "Hosanna." Now he is to be crucified on a hill outside the city walls, for Jewish law does not allow executions inside the city. Two criminals will also be crucified at the same time.

Crucifixion—the act of nailing a man to a wooden cross—is the standard Roman form of capital punishment. It is brutal. A man can take days to die, hanging alone on the cross until he wastes away. To this heinous death for Jesus is added the torment of dragging the cross through the streets of Jerusalem. Jesus staggers, trailed by a guard on horseback who is prepared to whip him if he falls or drops the cross.

Jesus is in agony as he struggles toward his death. His body is bent by the weight of the cross, and the crown of thorns inflicts a new burst of pain whenever the cross bumps against it. The many beatings he has endured make it hard to breathe, for his jailers have kicked and punched him in the ribs again and again.

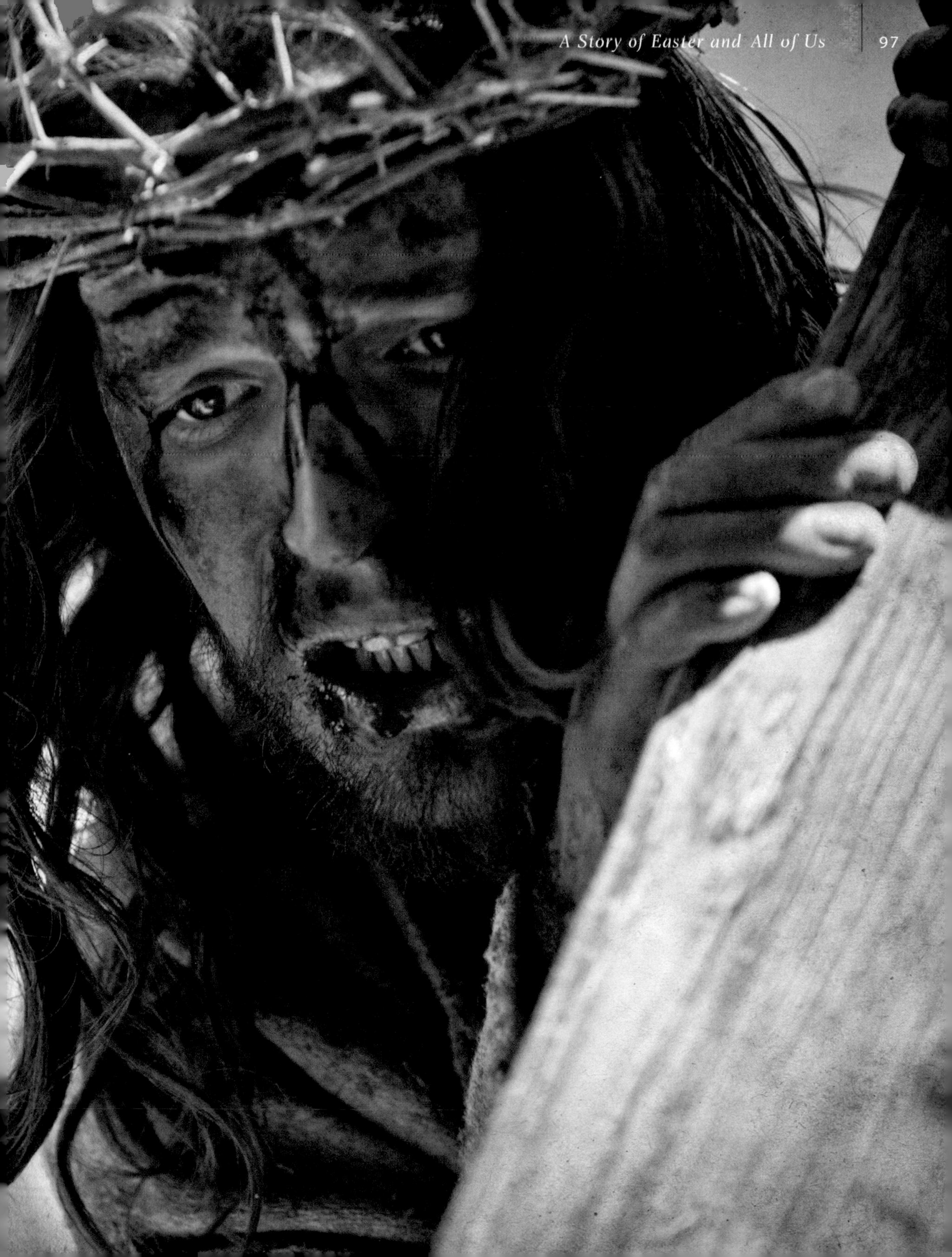

The ground is cobbled, so the cross bumps along rather than drags smoothly. The distance from Pilate's palace to Golgotha, the place where Jesus will die, is five hundred yards. Jesus knows he cannot make it. He spits out a gob of blood, falls to his knees, drops the cross, and crumples to the ground. Roman soldiers are upon him in an instant, raining kicks and punches on his helpless body. Mary races forward to save her son, but a Roman guard grabs her roughly and throws her back.

"Please!" John cries, risking his life by stepping from the crowd. "She's his mother!" Tears stream down Mary's cheeks. The Roman guard steps toward John with a menacing glare on his face, but the disciple is undeterred. "Have mercy, please!"

Mary can't help herself. She flings herself forward and falls onto her knees, next to her son. "My son!" she sobs as she wraps her arms lovingly around him in what will surely be their last embrace.

Jesus can hardly react, but forces his swollen eyes open. "Don't be afraid. The Lord is with you," he says through gasps, repeating exactly what the angel Gabriel had told her when he visited her as a young virgin. His words give her strength, and his look of love fills her with courage. She knows this is what he came to do.

Then suddenly Mary is pulled away from her son. The soldiers whip the fallen Jesus, but it is clear that he cannot carry the cross any farther. A man of obvious strength, Simon of Cyrene, is chosen and forced to shoulder the cross for Jesus. Their eyes lock, and then their hands link to lift the heavy wood. Together, they share the burden. Step by painful step, the two complete the long walk up to the crucifixion site.

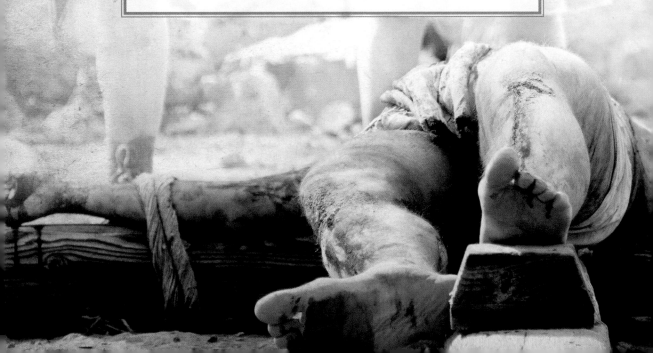

THE CROWD THINS as Jesus leaves the city walls behind. Mary, John, and Mary Magdalene walk to the side of the road as it curls steeply upward. This hill is known as Golgotha, the "Place of the Skulls," because it is believed that the skull of Adam is buried here.

Choking dust fills the air, and Jesus can barely breathe. He trips and is immediately whipped. He rises and then trips again. And once more, he immediately feels the sting of the lash.

Jesus and Simon the Cyrene finally arrive at the place of crucifixion. Simon drops the heavy cross and quickly leaves. Jesus, no longer able to stand, collapses into the dust. The Roman guards spring into action. Coils of rope are unwound and laid flat. Spades dig out the excess earth from the holes in the ground so often used for crucifixions.

"I want to see him," Mother Mary murmurs as she strains against the arms of a Roman guard who prevents her from getting close to Jesus.

Mary Magdalene sinks to her knees and starts to pray. Mother Mary stands resolutely upright, keeping a distant vigil over her son. John stands next to her, ready to catch her if she collapses from the stress.

Jesus is laid on the cross. The guards stretch out his arms and hammer nails into his hands. His feet are nailed to the cross, one over the other. The sound of his bones breaking fills the air, and Jesus gasps at each new burst of pain. After everything he's endured, nothing hurts like the moment the nails pierce his feet.

Despite Caiaphas's protest, Pilate's sign is nailed into the cross above Jesus' head: JESUS OF NAZARETH: KING OF THE JEWS.

JESUS OF NAZARETH
King of the Jews

To raise the cross, ropes are attached, one end to the cross and the other to the horse that will pull it to an upright position. A whip cracks, and the horse walks forward. Jesus no longer sees just the sky above. Now he sees all of Jerusalem in the distance, and his loving mother standing vigil at the base of the cross.

Jesus can barely breathe. His outstretched arms make it almost impossible to draw a breath. He knows he will suffocate. It is not the nails that kill, but the steady weakening of the body until it becomes impossible for the lungs to expand.

The cross is upright. Jesus hangs from it. The executioner's job is done. Those soldiers who crucified Jesus divide his clothes among them and cast lots for his garment. Meanwhile, those who have watched the crucifixion step forward.

Mother Mary weeps with unbearable grief.

"Come to save others but can't even save yourself," mocks a Pharisee.

Jesus hears it all. He moans, and then speaks to God: "Father, forgive them, for they know not what they do."

The two criminals have been crucified on either side of him. The first taunts Jesus: "Aren't you the Messiah? Why don't you save yourself and us?"

The second criminal responds, "Our punishment is just. But this man has done nothing wrong." He turns to Jesus and speaks softly. "Remember me, Messiah, when you come into your Kingdom."

Jesus turns to him, grimacing in pain. "Truly, I say to you, today you will be with me in Paradise."

The Romans won't go home until all three of the crucified men are dead. It's just a matter of time.

Mary, John, and Mary Magdalene stand at the base of Jesus' cross. He is immobile and seems dead. It is now midafternoon, almost time for the start of Passover, just before sunset. The Roman soldiers know that his body must be taken off the cross by then and are contemplating breaking his legs to kill him quicker, but they will not need to do that.

"My God, my God," Jesus cries out suddenly, "why have you forsaken me?" This is the first sentence of Psalm 22, King David's lament for the Jews and a cry for help. Then he looks down at Mary who stands, with silent tears running down her face. "Mother, this is your son," he tells her, referring to John as he stands at her side with a protective arm around her. "John," he adds, "this is your mother."

Jesus looks away, consumed by the pain, and then looks upward as a hard wind kicks up. A rumble of thunder sweeps across the land. "I thirst," Jesus says. In response, a soldier soaks a sponge and raises it up to his lips on a spear.

"My God, my God, why have you forsaken me?"

In a barely conscious fog of pain, Jesus hears more thunder. Black storm clouds now fill the sky as he knows that the time has come to leave this world. "It is finished!" Jesus cries aloud. "Father, into your hands I commend my spirit!"

The thunder strikes. This bundle of energy, vibration, and sheer power explodes upon Jerusalem. In the Temple, the great curtain is ripped in two, and panicked crowds race to flee the building, leaving their hard-earned sacrificial animals behind.

Mother Mary knows it is the signal that her son has died. She stares up at Jesus with a look of utter calm. All the pain she has been suffering is gone, replaced by the peace of realizing that her son will suffer no more.

The terrified Roman guards believe the thunder to be an omen, and they hurry to break the legs of the crucified so they can remove their bodies before Passover. They hastily grab metal rods and swing them hard against the two criminals on either side of Jesus. But they see that Jesus is already dead. To make sure, the Roman commander runs a spear through his side.

"He's dead," the commander confirms, pulling his spear out of Jesus. He looks across at Jesus' mother, then back up at Jesus, and slowly says, "Surely this man was the Son of God."

NORMALLY, THE BODIES of the crucified are left to rot or are thrown into shallow pits. But Nicodemus and Joseph of Arimathea have secured special permission from Pilate to take the body down and bury it decently. Tombs overlooking Jerusalem are normally reserved for the wealthiest citizens, but Joseph has arranged for an expensive, newly hewn tomb to be the final resting place of the Messiah. Typically, a tomb contained the bodies of several family members, but Jesus' body would be the first and only body to be laid there.

The two stately elders, the older Mary, the younger Mary, and John gingerly retrieve the mangled Messiah's body and prepare it for burial. His mother lovingly washes him with a sponge, cleaning away all the dirt and dried blood, while the other Mary tears strips of linen. Mother Mary places one over Jesus' face. Nicodemus anoints each cleansed portion of the body with fragrant oils and prays over Jesus the entire time. Then the process of wrapping his body in linen begins—a long emotional process, the official beginning of Jewish mourning.

A vast slab of stone is the opening of a cave, and Jesus' body, immaculately wrapped in linen, is placed inside on a hewn rock. Strong servants of Nicodemus and Joseph of Arimathea roll the rock over the opening of the tomb to make sure that the body won't be disturbed. Night has fallen, so the burial party lights torches to guide their way back down the path. As the group begins to leave, they are surprised to see Roman guards stepping forth to stand sentry. Pilate is fearful that if the body of Jesus disappears, all of Jerusalem will riot. Better to make sure it doesn't happen.

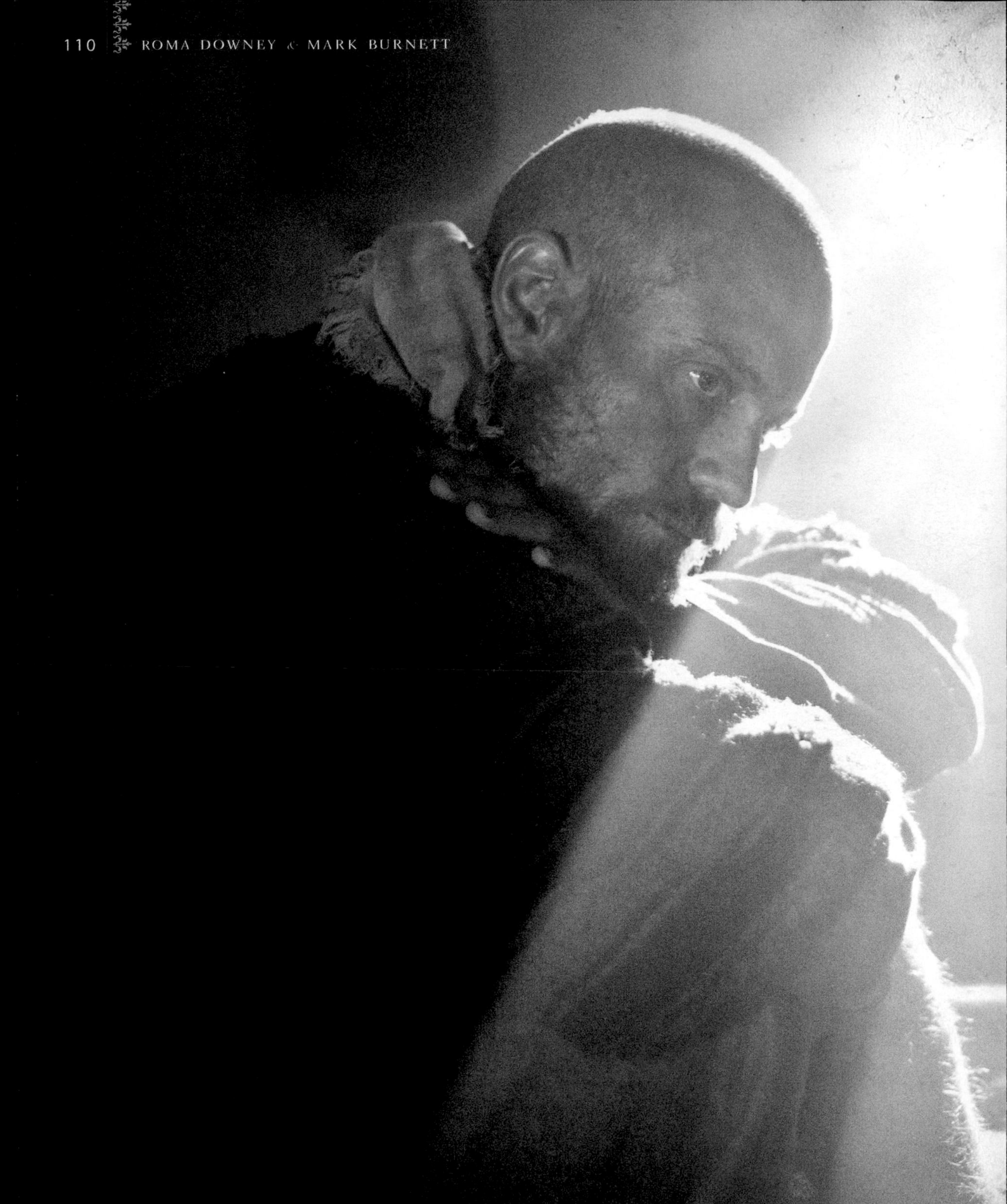

ALL OVER JERUSALEM, people are celebrating the Passover. But in the small upper room where Jesus and his disciples took their last meal, the mood is somber. The disciples expected the Kingdom of God to come when they entered Jerusalem six days ago. Now everything they believe in has been destroyed. Their hope is gone. They have lost everything. They eat a small quiet meal together, certain that within moments soldiers will come to arrest them.

THE MORNING OF THE THIRD DAY after Jesus' death, Mary Magdalene goes to visit the tomb. She misses Jesus enormously, and even the prospect of sitting outside his burial site is a source of comfort. As she ascends a small hill, she knows that even in the early morning fog she will be able to see the tomb from the top, and she begins looking once she gets there. The entrance to the tomb stands open! The rock has been moved aside. She gasps. Has someone stolen Jesus' body? Mary fearfully takes a step toward the open tomb but doesn't dare enter.

Mary weeps at the empty tomb and then, still sobbing, takes a deep breath and conquers her fears. It's pitch-black, but her eyes soon adjust. She sees the slab where Jesus' body was laid. The linens that were bound tightly around his body now lie in a pile. Mary smells the sweet perfume that was poured onto Jesus' corpse to minimize the smell of decay.

"Why are you crying?" asks a man's voice at the tomb's opening. "Who are you looking for?"

Mary can't see who's talking. Terrified she finds courage to call out from the darkness: "If you've taken him, tell me where he is."

"Mary."

It is the calm and knowing voice she knows all too well. Mary's heart soars as she realizes who is talking to her. "Jesus!" Her eyes swim with tears of joy and amazement as she steps out into the sunlight.

"Go and tell our brothers I am here."

Mary stares at Jesus in awe. She can see the spike marks on his hands and feet. There is an aura about Jesus, something far more heavenly than anything she has experienced in all their many days together. It is as though she is looking at two sides of the same being: God and man. Then he is gone. Overcome with joy, Mary sprints back into Jerusalem to tell the disciples the good news.

SINCE JESUS' EXECUTION, the disciples have been terrified that the religious authorities and Romans are working in unison to end all traces of Jesus' ministry, including them. They are hiding, fearful of the knock on the door telling them that they've been discovered.

Peter glances out a window. He is a shell of the man he once was, and no one would confuse him for the gruff fisherman Jesus recruited three years ago. Roman soldiers march up a nearby alley, breastplates and swords glistening in the early morning sun.

There is no knock at the door. Instead, Mary Magdalene suddenly bursts inside, screaming at the top of her lungs. "I've seen him! I've seen him!"

"Close the door!" barks John.

Mary slams it shut. "The tomb is open!" she gasps. "He's gone!"

"He's dead and buried," mutters a morose Peter. "That's impossible."

"You have to believe me. I saw him!"

"You must have been at the wrong tomb," states Thomas. "It has to be someone else."

"You don't think I know what Jesus looks like? Do you think I'm mad?"

"Mary, calm down. This has been stressful for all of us."

This infuriates her. She grips Peter's wrist hard and pulls him to the door. "Come with me. Now!"

Peter looks to John, then at the other disciples. It wouldn't be safe for all of them to venture out, but perhaps just two of them. He nods, and Mary leads him and John out into the sunshine.

THEY STARE IN SHOCK and disbelief at the empty tomb. Peering sheepishly inside from a few feet back, they can't see any signs that tomb robbers had been there, but that seems the obvious answer.

Peter steps into the opening, then into the empty tomb, where he sees the burial cloth and strips of linen and takes them into his hands. With a sudden sense of knowing, he realizes that Mary's words are true. Stunned, Peter steps back out of the tomb.

Mary sees the look on his face. "Now do you believe me?" she asks.

Peter hands John a strip of linen from the tomb. "But he's gone," John says, mystified.

"No, my brother," Peter assures him, that old confidence suddenly returned. "He is not gone. He's back!" An exuberant Peter takes off and races down the hill. On the way, he purchases a loaf of bread from a vendor.

"What happened?" asks Matthew as the three of them step back inside the hiding place.

"A cup," Peter answers. "I need a cup."

Peter gives a piece of unleavened bread to John, who puts it slowly into his mouth. "His body," Peter reminds him. A cup is found and thrust into John's hand. Peter fills it with wine and says, "And his blood."

Suddenly transformed into the rock of faith Jesus always knew he could be, Peter looks from disciple to disciple. "Believe in him. He's here. In this room. Right now."

John drinks deeply from the cup as Peter continues talking. "Remember what he told us: 'I am the way, the truth—'"

"'And the life,'" Jesus finishes the sentence.

Peter spins around. Jesus stands in the doorway. The disciples are awestruck as he walks into the room.

"Peace be with you," Jesus, the risen Messiah, tells them.

"No," exclaims Thomas, "this is impossible! There is no way you are Jesus standing here with us. This is all a fantasy, an apparition brought on by our insane mourning for a man we loved so very much."

Jesus walks to Thomas and takes his hand. "Thomas, stop doubting and believe." He places Thomas's fingers into the gaping holes in his hands and then to the hole in his side.

Looking down, Thomas can clearly see the awful spike marks atop Jesus' feet, but he doesn't know how to respond. He knows Jesus' voice and appearance as well as he knows his own, but Thomas is a man of facts—a man committed to truth that cannot be disputed by emotion or trickery. He is being asked to believe that he is touching Jesus, as alive as the last time they all broke bread together in the upper room. It seems impossible, but it is real. This is Jesus, not some dream or vision. Thomas touches the wounds and hears his teacher's voice. Overwhelmed, Thomas looks into Jesus' eyes. "My Lord and my God," he stammers, tears filling his eyes. "It *is* you!"

Jesus looks at his disciple with compassion. "You believed because you see me. But blessed are those who have not seen me, and yet have believed."

Faith floods Thomas's entire being as he slowly accepts what it means to believe that anything is possible through God. This is the faith in Jesus that will transform lives—not seeing and yet still believing.

THE DISCIPLES SOON LEARN that Jesus is not here to stay. His work on earth—to die on the cross as a sacrifice for the sins of all men—is complete. Throughout history, millions of lambs have been slaughtered foreshadowing the same purpose. Jesus is the Lamb of God, who takes away the sins of the world. He has conquered sin and death.

Jesus appears to his disciples one last time before ascending into heaven. The disciples had fished all night but caught nothing, until the early morning when Jesus, whom they didn't recognize, called to them from shore and told them to try the right side of the boat, resulting in an amazing catch of more than one hundred and fifty large fish. Realizing it was Jesus, and being invited by him to share breakfast, they join him to eat, and he speaks to them of the future.

Twice during the discussion Jesus asks Peter: "Do you love me?" Both times, Peter responds with a surprised yes, and Jesus instructs him to feed his lambs and take care of his sheep. When Jesus asks a third time, Peter is hurt. But he also knows he had denied Jesus three times, so these responses have been his moment of redemption. "Lord," Peter sighs, "you know all things. You know that I love you."

"Feed my sheep," Jesus tells him a third time. "Follow me!"

Forty days after his resurrection, Jesus says good-bye to his disciples. For three full years he has trained them and equipped them with the skills to lead others to follow in his footsteps and worship God. "You will receive power when the Holy Spirit comes to you," he tells them. "My body can be in only one place, but my spirit can be with you all wherever you are. Go into the world and preach the gospel to all creation."

The disciples know this is the last time they will see Jesus. He is not saying that the Holy Spirit will come into them right now, so they must wait for this great moment. Everything he said would happen has come to pass, and it is clear that the power of God extends much further than they even dared to believe. They have nothing to fear—even death.

"Peace be with you," says Jesus.

The words echo in the disciples' ears. This peace pulses through them, infusing them with energy and calm resolve—this is the peace that will fortify them as they do God's work.

As the disciples watch, Jesus then ascends into heaven.

The disciples feel the loss, as Jesus' physical presence among them is no more. Peter's eyes fill with tears as he tilts his head upward. He blinks away his tears and feels his breath return, then stands to address the other disciples. He knows that Jesus will always be with them and with all people. He has accepted Jesus' command that he follow him, no matter what the cost. Now it is time to go out into the world and let the people know about the greatness of God.

"Be strong, my brothers," says Peter, his voice sure and brave. "We have work to do—a world to change."

a world to change.

Books and resources based on

THE BIBLE
EPIC MINISERIES

A Story of God and All of Us, "Novel"

A Story of God and All of Us, "100 Daily Reflections"

A Story of Christmas and All of Us

A Story of Easter and All of Us

THE BIBLE the Epic Miniseries, "Blu-ray and DVD"

THE BIBLE, "Music Inspired by the Epic Miniseries"

THE BIBLE, "The Official Soundtrack"

THE BIBLE, "30-Day Experience
for Churches and Small Groups"